POINTS IN TIME

Ecco Press
Books by Paul Bowles

The Delicate Prey *(Stories)*

A Distant Episode *(Stories)*

Jean Genet in Tangier *by Mohamed Choukri*
(Translation)

Points in Time *(Fiction)*

Their Heads Are Green and Their Hands Are Blue
(Essays)

Up Above the World *(Novel)*

Without Stopping *(Autobiography)*

About Paul Bowles

An Invisible Spectator *by Christopher Sawyer-Lauçanno*
(Biography)

Paul Bowles

POINTS
IN
TIME

The Ecco Press
New York

First published by The Ecco Press in 1984
26 West 17th Street, New York, NY 10011
Published simultaneously in Canada by
George J. McLeod, Limited, Toronto
Published by arrangement with Peter Owen, Limited
Printed in the United States of America

Library of Congress Cataloging in Publication Data

Bowles, Paul Frederic, 1911-
Points in time.

Reprint. Originally published:
London: P. Owen, 1982.
Includes bibliographical references.
1. Morocco—History—Fiction.   I. Title.

PS3552.0874P6   1984   813'.54   83-16571
ISBN 0-88001-044-4

After half a day's voyage they came to a large lake or marsh. No such place now exists, the lagoons being all to the north of the cape. South of it the shore is either guarded by cliffs, steep slopes, or stony and sandy beaches.

Nor is there any sign of such a lake having existed, and the sudden winter rains which make every dry watercourse roar from bank to bank are not of a character fit to cause floods likely to be mistaken for a marsh or a lake.

He dreamed of a hawk that hovered. A warning, the others said. And they went down to Asana, and a blind man at the entrance to the city raised his hand and spoke.

Pay heed to the wind that moves above this place. The drums you hear are not of our people, nor are the hands that hit the skins.

He saw the blind man's face and remembered the hawk. Behind the walls and higher were the hills, white and hard against the noonday sky.

And they did not enter Asana, but turned southward over an empty plain, and came to the bank of a river.

Asana was destroyed. Only dust was there.

Another road led from Tocolosida to Tingis. The first-named place is doubtful. It might have been Mghila or Zarhun, but it was neither Amergo nor Ksar Faraun. The stones of Tocolosida are there in the shadows below the cliff.

The Moorish Sultan (who had suffered at Sierra Morena such a defeat by the Spaniards that for several days the victors used no other fuel than the pikes, lances and arrows of their fallen enemies) answered his captors with great dignity that he had lately read the Book of Paul's Epistles, which he liked so much that were he to choose another faith it should be Christianity.

But for his part (Nazarenes have the minds of small children) he thought every man should die in the religion into which he was born. (And this will probably not get through into those pork-nourished brains.) The only fault I find with Paul is that he deserted Judaism, he told them, smiling.

The old cemetery by the grottoes has been despoiled. To our great grief they have converted it into ploughed land. And by the seven sefarim and the seven heavens, by the twelve roes, by the bread and the salt, by the Name and the sacrifice, we swear that justice shall be made to prevail.

A few can remember that summer. The sun's breath shrivelled what it touched. No one went out, for there was fever in the lower city.

They say he had a walled-in garden where he walked at sunset. It could have been his prison, save that he was free, and with the leisure to invent the perils that beset him from within. 'Shall the pillar of the law be shattered, and the edifice laid with the dust, the Mishnah desecrated and trodden underfoot?' With the seven categories of the just may his part and lot remain.

No one went out. We waited in our darkened rooms, and with every breath of wind that clicked the blinds we shuddered. May those destroyed by fever rest in Eden, and their dwelling be under the Tree of Life.

II

In the course of his travels in Portugal, Fra Andrea of Spoleto had met a man for whom he felt great sympathy, and the man happened to be a Moslem. Heretofore he had not known anyone professing that faith, none having chanced to visit the Franciscan monastery where he had lived, and he was amazed, after an hour's talk with this Moroccan gentleman, to find him not only wholly conversant with Christian doctrine, but actually in accord with certain of its tenets.

They saw one another often during that year. As a result of their growing friendship, Si Musa conceived the idea of inviting Fra Andrea to Fez, in order to set up a small Franciscan mission there. Initially the concept struck the monk as purely a fantasy, and quite unrealizable. Then Si Musa let fall the information that his wife was the sister of King Mohammed VIII who at that time ruled Morocco from Fez.

As you know, His Majesty has had ample opportunity to study the works of the Christians, Si Musa remarked with a wry smile. Fra Andrea nodded; he understood that his friend was referring to the unfortunate king's long incarceration by the Portuguese.

Solitude and study can make a man tolerant, you know, he went on. It would give him great pleasure to have you and your friends in Fez, so that the public could see for itself that not all infidels are savages.

Here Fra Andrea guffawed. Si Musa smiled politely, not understanding the reason for his mirth. It was this very ingenuousness in the Moroccan which delighted the monk, and which doubtless was instrumental in persuading him to accept his unlikely suggestion.

Three years later Fra Andrea arrived in Fez, along with Fra Antonio and Fra Giacomo, two other Franciscans who had gone because they considered it their duty to be on hand in Fez, where they might be able to intercede on behalf of Christian hostages being held for ransom. Fra Andrea was looking forward particularly to having religious discussions with the several Moslem intellectuals to whom Si Musa had given him letters of introduction.

From the moment of their arrival everything went wrong for the three. When Fra Andrea tried to find the men to whom he had the notes, he discovered that they were all mysteriously absent from Fez. The old palace near the Fondouq Nejjarine which Si Musa had assured him would be put at his disposal proved not to be available. Indeed, the mere mention of Si Musa's name brought forth unfriendly stares.

It did not take him long to learn the reason. While they had been en route to Fez a new monarch had been crowned: King Ahmed III. The friars received this news with inexpressive faces, but among themselves they discussed it dolefully, agreeing that it did not bode well for their project.

They were advised to look for a house in Fez Djedid, where foreigners were not regarded with quite such antipathy as in the Medina. The house they found was not far from the entrance to the Mellah. It had only three small rooms, but there was a patio, which they soon filled with potted plants.

Fra Antonio and Fra Giacomo quickly accustomed themselves to the static life of their new dwelling. They seemed to be contented in the dreary little house. But Fra Andrea was restless; he had been counting on passing long hours in the company of new friends with whom he could talk.

The few excursions he made into the Medina persuaded him that he would do better to stay out of it. Thus he took to wandering in the Mellah, where it is true that he was stared at with much the same hostility as in the Medina, the difference being that he was not afraid of the Jews. He did not believe that they would attack him physically, even though they must have felt considerable rancour towards his Church for the recent deportations of Jews from Spain. Fra Andrea considered theirs a politically motivated hostility, whereas the hatred he had encountered in the Medina transcended such considerations. He felt free to walk in the alleys of the Mellah, and to listen to the Spanish conversation of the passers-by.

One evening as he stood leaning against a wall, enjoying the scraps of domestic conversation that reached him from inside the houses, a portly gentleman came along the alley, saw him standing there, and bade him good evening. Embarrassed at having been caught eavesdropping, Fra Andrea replied briefly and started to walk away.

The other spoke again, and pointed at a door. This was his house, he said, and he invited him to come in. Only when the monk stood inside a well-lighted room did he see that his host was a rabbi.

In this way Fra Andrea came to know Rabbi Harun ben Hamu and to pay him regular visits. He had found a Moroccan with whom he might conceivably have religious and metaphysical discussions. Rabbi Harun ben Hamu was exceedingly courteous, and showed a willing-

19

ness to engage in serious conversation, but Fra Andrea felt the need to study the Talmud carefully before expressing any opinions touching on Judaic law. He could read Hebrew haltingly, and this small knowledge gained early in life served him perfectly in his present project.

For more than a year he spent most of his time in intensive study. He filled a book with notations and learned the Mishnah by heart. During this time he paid constant visits to the rabbi's house, where eventually he was presented to two other men, Rabbi Judah ibn Danan and Rabbi Shimon Saqali. He saw that these two did not entirely accept the presence of an anonymous Christian friar in their midst, and this gave him a powerful desire to impress them. It was hard for him to sit by and be silent when he was so eager to discuss their religion with them, but he was preparing himself for the day when he would be able to meet them on an equal footing in the arena of religious polemics, so he held his tongue.

When he had decided that he knew the Law as well as they knew it, and perhaps understood its relation to Islam and Christianity rather better than they, he determined to speak on the next occasion when they should find themselves together.

He had not been wrong in expecting them to show incredulity and amazement when he began to address them. They listened, nodding their heads slowly, puzzled by his strange metamorphosis. At one point he remarked that the halakkic material had little to do with God, and that even the haggadic midrashim contained no passages dealing with the nature of God.

Rabbi Shimon Saqali stiffened. Every phrase contains an infinite number of meanings, he said.

And an infinite number of meanings is equivalent to no meaning at all! cried Fra Andrea. Then, seeing the expressions on the faces of the three men, he decided to

20

make a joke of it, and laughed, but this seemed only to mystify them.

As the discussion progressed, he found in himself a strong desire to confound them, to confront them with their own contradictions. He had behind him years of practice in the art of theological argument, and this had given him an extraordinary memory. He could recall the exact words which had come from the lips of each man during the evening, and he quoted them accurately, his eye on the one who had uttered them.

Even Rabbi Harun ben Hamu was astounded, not so much by his friend's sudden burst of erudition as by his masterly use of logic. Rabbi Shimon and Rabbi Judah were appalled by Fra Andrea; after he had left they told their host as much. Never before had they been baited and humiliated in such a manner, they declared.

Rabbi Harun, who felt mildly possessive about his foreign friend, tried to reassure them. The Christian meant no offence, he told them. He's not one of us, after all.

Then, as they made no answer, he added: a brilliant man.

Yes, unnaturally brilliant, said Rabbi Judah.

Fra Andrea walked back to his house that night highly satisfied with the effect he had produced upon his listeners. Strangely enough, Rabbi Harun ben Hamu continued to invite the other two rabbis and the monk together, and they continued to meet around his table. After his first indiscretion Fra Andrea was careful not to express his personal opinions regarding the Talmud. The discussions were limited to Christian theology. With his diabolically clever mind and tongue Fra Andrea invariably silenced the others. Rabbi Harun ben Hamu greatly enjoyed being host to these fiery harangues. And little by little he found himself accepting many of the monk's premises. The other two noticed with misgiving his growing tendency to agree with him in small matters. This troubled them, and in private they discussed it.

One evening as they sat around Rabbi Harun ben Hamu's table, Fra Andrea in passing thoughtlessly qualified the Targumim as inaccurate and inexcusably vulgar exegeses. Rabbi Judah smote the table with his fist, but this warning sign escaped Fra Andrea's notice.

The Targum to the Megilloth, for instance, he continued, is a piece of unparalleled nonsense. How can anyone credit such absurdities?

Then with great gusto he proceeded to demolish the Second Targum of Esther, not heeding the pallid rigidity in the faces of both Rabbi Judah and Rabbi Shimon.

All at once Rabbi Judah laid his hand on Rabbi Shimon's arm. As one man they rose and left the house. Fra Andrea ceased to speak, looking to Rabbi Harun for an explanation. But his host was staring straight ahead, an expression of mingled doubt and terror on his face.

Fra Andrea waited. Slowly Rabbi Harun raised his head and as if in supplication pointed to the door. Please, he said.

He did not rise from the table when his guest went out. He understood that the other two rabbis had come to the conclusion that the monk was in league with Satan. Although Rabbi Harun ben Hamu was a fairly learned man, the possibility of such a thing did not seem to him at all unlikely. He resolved that under no circumstances would he see the Christian again.

It never became necessary for him to implement his decision. Two days later all the notables and elders of the Mellah (save Rabbi Harun ben Hamu, whom his colleagues considered to be already contaminated by the power of evil) went in a procession to the palace. There they protested at the presence in Fez of a foreign sorcerer

22

who had been sent to sow discord among their people. They charged Fra Andrea with 'conspiracy and the practice of magic'.

The Moslems, only too happy to have a pretext for ridding their city of this undesirable Christian, agreed to arrest him.

Fra Andrea was given no opportunity of defending himself against the charges, but was thrown straightway into a cell where they tortured him for a few hours. Finally someone impaled his body on a lance.

III

The Armada lay under the water, and the land of Spain lay above, colour of camels and saffron.

Shoubilia, Gharnatta, Kortoba, Magherit, fell under the years, to be remembered at dusk by exiles in Fez.

Then Ahmed IV, the Emperor of Morocco, sent a message to Charles I, telling of his success (illusory) in dealing with the pirates of Slâ, and suggesting the need of British aid in combating those of Algeria and Tunis.

The Moriscos of Andalucía had made every concession, undergone every indignity, even to being baptized, eating turnips in public, and wearing crucifixes, in the hope of avoiding exile.

Notwithstanding, the Inquisition did not consider their conversion a genuine one, and continued to deport them to Slâ and Rabat where, since they spoke no Arabic, they were at a great disadvantage.

Here the sun was hotter and the waves higher than at home in Almería or Motril.

The fishing, at least, was good.

At night, in the boats, the men could talk.

Every second, ten stars set behind the black water in the west.

When we went out in several boats, we spoke of revenge. What would it be like if a Spanish ship appeared and we were to overtake it and climb aboard? How would we make ourselves happy?

One day such a ship did come along, sailing straight in our direction.

By the time they saw us, it was too late for them to change the course of the ship, and we caught up with them easily, every man pulling on the oars with all his strength.

Then we shouted: *Allah akbar*! and went onto the ship.

Only three of our men were lost. We finished off all the Spaniards, took what we could into the boats, and went back to the port.

Now that we had seen their blood, we felt better.

The ship drifted ashore farther south.

Soon we had good luck again, but this time the ship was British. We knew better than to kill any more than we had to.

Instead of cutting up the crew and the passengers, we bound them and carried them back to Slâ. The prices they fetched were a gift from Allah.

Little by little we gave up fishing. We were spending all

28

our time building faster boats.

When the men of Slâ saw this, they set to work doing the same thing.

The seas are full of Nazarene ships, they said. There are enough for all. It is pleasing to the Most High that the riches of the infidels should be returned to Islam.

The Sultan writes to the kings in Europe: he deplores the slave traffic, Marrakech lies at a considerable distance from Slâ, he is unable to do away with the lawlessness there, notwithstanding the great effort he is putting forth in his attempt to abolish piracy.

He does not tell them that he collects one guirch for every ten realized by the trade.

In Fez it is said that Moslems spend most of their money on weddings, Jews on Pesagh, and Christians on lawsuits. But what the people of Fez call lawsuits are the frantic attempts by Europeans to secure the audience of local dignitaries willing to help them arrange the payment of ransom for their relatives and countrymen being held as hostages.

The Sultan wrote to the British.

'Praise be to the Most High alone! And Allah's blessing be upon those who are for his prophet.

'As for those men thou didst say were taken at sea, I neither know nor have heard anything of them.

'Our servant, Mohammed ben Hadu Aater, who came from your presence, told us that lions are scarce in your country, and that they are in high estimation with you. When your servant came to us, he found we had two small young lions; wherefore by him we send them to you.'

Heavy sea and a gale from the east.

An English privateer sailed into the bay at daybreak. We dispatched four men to bring the ship into harbour. Then we all went quickly to the shore at the foot of the cliffs and waited.

When the prow hit the reef we swam out and climbed aboard. Some of the passengers dived into the water.

The captain and the crew were on deck. This time we had orders to kill as few as possible. We took them all alive save for one English woman who drowned when she jumped overboard.

We had the chains ready, and we drove them ahead of us through Tangier.

That night there was more wind and rain, and our tents were spread on the sand at the edge of the Oued Tahadartz.

Three at a time we brought in the crew, and they sat with their chains in our tent.

Abdeslam ben Larbi spoke with them in their tongue. Embrace the true faith, and you need not be slaves.

A few screamed curses, but the rest agreed.

They were poor youths, not likely to be ransomed.

During the last hour of darkness they were unshackled and silently taken across the river. We did not see them again.

When daybreak came we set out with our captives. To be safe, we took away their heavy footgear. They walked barefoot like us, and protested greatly, claiming that it caused them much pain.

Each day more of the prisoners had bloody and swollen feet. Some could no longer walk, and we left them behind. Had it taken many days more to reach Meknes, we should have lost them all.

The conquests of Emanuel the Fortunate mention the capture of Azamur, where the sun shone strong on the fort's low tower. Hot lead splashed down the sluices. Get back! cried the crowd. Later they made the finest drums of any town along the coast. 'And no Christian was permitted to ride into the city on horseback, or Jew enter it except barefooted (as in Fez and other cities to this day).'

The same day thither there came aboard of us a young gentleman of that country. He had fled from his father, having had the misfortune to kill his elder brother, whom his father loved entirely.

In the courtyard. By the fountain. There was no time. I heard my father at the door. Not even time to pull out the knife. Only to hide and then run out of the house. Allah! Allah!

This young gentleman was much given to repeating the doleful account of his misfortune, amid divers piteous lamentations, and all this in such great measure that our good Captain was constrained to lock him away in the dark below, where he passed the entire voyage. It is well to remember that the Morocco pirates learnt their trade from the English rovers driven out of the European area.

And the Sultan wrote to the British.

'And know that we have received, by our servants, from your master, three coach horses; now a coach requires four horses to draw it, wherefore you must needs send us another good one of the same kind and size, that they may draw the coach with four horses. Oblige us in this, by all means. Farewell! We depend upon it. Written on the seventh of the sacred month of Du El Kadah, in the year ninety-three and a thousand.'

IV

The sound of the sea on the wind blowing through the streets of Essaouira today is the same as it was two hundred years ago, when Andrew Layton had a small exporting business there, together with two Frenchmen, Messieurs Secard and Barre. The three men often set out on their horses into the countryside roundabout, Layton's greyhounds accompanying them. There were very few Europeans in the town, so that these excursions had become their favourite pastime.

One day the three, along with a clerk who worked in their office, went out of the town on their horses. To escape the wind they rode inland, rather than skirting the dunes to the south. Their route led them past several small Chleuh villages. The dogs raced here and there across the scrubland. They passed a hamlet where men and women were working in the fields, while cows grazed nearby. The greyhounds rushed onto the scene and made a concerted attack upon the cattle. As a calf fell, a farmer in the field raised his gun and shot one of the dogs. The others scattered.

The Europeans had seen. They rode up and dismounted, but before they had even begun to speak, the field-workers were hurling stones at them. Monsieur Barre received the most serious bruises. A general mêlée ensued, in the course of which Layton and his associates made free use of their riding-whips. Then they turned and galloped back to Essaouira in a state of high indignation. The occurrence was unusual, and by their standards, outrageous. They went immediately to see the Pacha.

To appease the Europeans, with whom he was on friendly terms, the Pacha first advised them henceforth to ride southward along the beach, notwithstanding the wind, rather than going inland past the villages. Then he agreed to call in the offending farmers. The following day a large group of them appeared in the town. They were in a state of great excitement, and straightway began a frenzied clamour for retribution. A village woman was missing two teeth, which she insisted that Layton had broken. Again and again the villagers called, in the name of Allah and the Prophet, for justice.

Perplexed by the turn events had taken, the Pacha decided to refer the matter to the Sultan. In due course a reply came from His Majesty, ordering all the parties concerned to report to the palace at Marrakech.

At the hearing, which finally took place in the presence of the Sultan, Layton was ingenuous enough to give a straightforward account of the incident. Included was his admission that he had struck the woman in the face with the butt of his whip, thus breaking two of her incisors. He offered to make monetary payment, but the villagers were adamant in their refusal. They had not come to Marrakech expecting money, they declared. What they demanded was precise retaliation: Layton must furnish them with two of his own teeth. Nothing else was acceptable.

Since the peasants were within their rights in asking that the law of the land be applied, the Sultan had no choice but to order the extractions to be performed then and there. The official tooth-puller stepped forward, ready to start. Layton, although considerably disconcerted, had the presence of mind to ask that the teeth to be pulled be two molars which recently had been giving him trouble. The complainants agreed to the suggestion. Back teeth being larger and heavier than front teeth, they felt that they were getting the better of the bargain.

The operation went ahead under the intent scrutiny of the villagers. They were waiting to hear the infidel's cries of pain. Layton, however, preserved a stoical silence throughout the ordeal. The molars were washed and presented to the claimants, who went away entirely satisfied.

The Sultan had watched the proceedings with growing interest, and he arranged to hold a private conversation with Layton on the following day, when he apologized, at the same time expressing his admiration for the Englishman's fortitude. He could scarcely do less, he said, than agree to grant whatever favour his guest might ask of him.

Layton replied that he desired only that the permit to export a cargo of wheat from Essaouira be expedited. His modesty and candour impelled the monarch to take a personal interest in him, and the two became fast friends.

It was the Emperor's hope that Layton might eventually be persuaded to accept the post of British Consul in Marrakech. There at least, he argued, he would not have to contend with the wind. But the prospect did not appeal to Layton, who preferred to continue his life at Essaouira with his horses and dogs. He had got used to the wind, he said.

V

Whenever his own tribe won a victory in a battle with another tribe, Si Abdallah el Hassoun inwardly rejoiced. At the same time he considered this pleasure a base emotion, one unworthy of him. Thus, to fortify his sanctity he bade farewell to his students and went to live in Slâ, which is by the sea.

It was not long before the divinity students of his school sent several of their number to Si Abdallah, imploring him to return to them. Without replying, the saint led them to the rocks at the edge of the sea.

How turbulent the water is! he exclaimed. The students agreed. Then Si Abdallah filled a jar with the water and set it on a rock. Yet the water in here is still, he said, pointing at the jar. Why?

A student answered: Because it has been taken out of the place where it was.

Now you see why I must stay here, Si Abdallah said.

For thousands of afternoons in the Fondouq Askour, while the whores squabbled and shrieked in the courtyard outside his room, Sidi Moussa ed Douqqali worked at his obsessive task. He hoped to make asphodel stalks edible, but he died without having succeeded.

Sidi bel Abbes es Sebti was only fifteen when, realizing that he was a saint, he went to Marrakech to live a saint's life. For forty years he walked through the streets of the medina, wearing only a pair of serrouelles, while he extolled the virtues of poverty. He was known for the foul language he used in upbraiding those who took issue with him.

Sidi Belyout, tamer of wild beasts, was never to be seen without his entourage of pet lions. And Sidi Abderrahman el Mejdoub, who dealt in epigram and prophecy, was not only a saint. He was also mentally deranged, thus in direct natural contact with the source of all knowledge.

Along the Oued Tensift beyond the walls, there were caves that had been hollowed in the red earth cliffs. The entrance to Sidi Youssef's cave was protected by high thorn bushes and could not be seen from the river. He sought solitude, and although he was known for his great holiness, the people of Marrakech granted him his privacy, for he had leprosy. He claimed that the disease had been conferred upon him by Allah as a reward for his piety. When pieces of his flesh caught on the thorns and remained hanging there, he gave heartfelt thanks for these extra proofs of divine favour.

There were days when the students trembled. Are you cold? the master said.

We should sit in the courtyard, they told him. There are djenoun in hiding here.

Sidi Ali ben Harazem rebuked them, saying: Be still. If the prayers we send to Allah can reach the darker world, friends can be made from enemies, and Islam can enter there.

And the students shivered and wrote, hearing the water's gurgle beneath the tiles. And Sidi Ali ben Harazem talked until dusk, when the swallows no longer flew above the city.

VI

A century and a half ago, in one of the twisting back streets of the Mellah in Fez, there lived a respectable couple, Haim and Simha Hachuel. There would be no record of them today had their daughter Sol not been favoured with exceptional beauty.

Since Jewish girls were free to walk in the streets unveiled, the beauty of Sol Hachuel soon became legendary throughout the city.

Moslem youths climbed up from the Medina to stroll through the Mellah in the hope of catching sight of Sol on her way to a fountain to fetch water.

Having seen her once, Mohammed Zrhouni came each day and waited until she appeared, merely to gaze upon her. Later he spoke with her, and still later suggested that they marry.

Sol's parents rejected the idea outright: it would entail her abandonment of Judaism.

The Zrhouni family likewise strongly disapproved: they did not want a Jewess in the house, and they believed, like most Moslems, that no Jew's conversion to Islam could be considered authentic.

Mohammed was not disposed in any case to take a Moslem bride, since that would involve accepting the word of his female relatives as to the girl's desirability; by

51

the time he was finally able to see her face, he would already be married to her. Since the considerations of his family would necessarily be based on the bride-price, he strongly doubted that any girl chosen by them could equal the jewel he had discovered in the Mellah.

For her part, Sol was infatuated with her Moslem suitor. Her parents' furious tirades only increased the intensity of her obsession. Like Mohammed, she saw no reason to let herself be swayed by the opinions of her elders.

The inevitable occurred: she went out of the house one day and did not return. Mohammed covered her with a haik and went with her down into the Medina and across the bridge to his parents' house in the Keddane.

Mohammed lived with his mother, aunts and sisters, his father having died the previous year. Out of deference to him the women of the household received his bride with correctness, if not enthusiasm, and the wedding, with its explicit conversion of the bride to Islam, was performed.

His mother remarked in an aside to Mohammed that at least the bride had cost nothing, and he understood that this was the principal reason for her grudging acceptance of Sol as her daughter-in-law.

Almost immediately Sol realized that she had made an error. Although she was conversant with Moslem customs, it had not occurred to her that she would be forbidden ever to go outside the Zrhouni house.

When she remonstrated with Mohammed, saying that she needed to go out for a walk in the fresh air, he answered that it was common knowledge that a woman goes out only three times during her life: once when she is born and leaves her mother's womb, once when she marries and leaves her father's house, and once when she dies and leaves this world. He advised her to walk on the roof like other women.

The aunts and sisters, instead of coming little by little to accept Sol as a member of the family, made her feel increasingly like an interloper. They whispered among themselves and grew silent when they saw her approaching.

The months went by. Sol pleaded to be allowed to visit her mother and father. They could not come to see her, since the house would be profaned by their presence.

It seemed unjust to Sol that women were not allowed to enter the mosque; if only it had been possible to go with Mohammed and pray, her life would have been easier to bear. She missed the regular visits to the synagogue where she sat upstairs with her mother and listened to her father as he chanted below with the other men.

The Zrhouni house had become a prison, and she resolved to escape from it. Accordingly, one day when she had managed to get hold of the key to the outer door, she wrapped herself in her haik and quietly slipped out into the street. Not looking to right or to left, she hurried up the Talâa to the top, and then set out for the Mellah.

The happiness in the Hachuel home lasted one day. Enraged and humiliated by his wife's dereliction, Mohammed had gone directly to the ulema and told them the story. They listened, consulted together, and declared his wife to be guilty of apostasy from Islam.

On the following afternoon a squad of mokhaznia pounded on the door of the house in the Mellah, and amid shrieks and lamentations, seized the girl. They pulled her out of the house and dragged her through the streets of Fez Djedid, with a great crowd following behind.

Outside Bab Segma the crowd spread out and formed a circle. Screaming and struggling against the ropes that bound her, Sol was forced to kneel in the dust.

A tall mokhazni unsheathed his sword, raised it high in the air, and beheaded her.

VII

Days of less substance than the nights that slipped between. And in the streets they whispered: Where is he? The murmuring filled the souq at sunset as the goods were stacked away.

In irons. In Fez.

Abdeljbar.

Raised eyebrows, swift smiles, nods of understanding. For when the Riffians had burned a Nazarene ship, Sultan Abderrahman, hoping to placate the owners, had sent his soldiers to the Rif. They went directly to the caids and cheikhs, offering silver *reales* in exchange for the names of the guilty ones.

In the town where Cheikh Abdeljbar lived there was a youth named El Aroussi, admired by everyone for the strength in his body and the beauty of his features. For some unexplained reason Cheikh Abdeljbar detested the young man, and this was the subject of many discussions in the souq. It was difficult to find the cause of his hostility.

Those who most disliked the cheikh said it was probable that at some time El Aroussi had repulsed the older man's attempts to seduce him. Others believed that, being of a jealous disposition, the cheikh could not forgive the youth for the many qualities Allah had bestowed upon him – particularly those qualities which made the girls and women wait for hours behind their lattices in order to see him walk by. People admired El Aroussi; they did not admire the cheikh.

El Aroussi knew nothing of the burned ship, and the cheikh was quite aware of this. All the same he named the youth as one of the raiders. El Aroussi was manacled and dragged off to a dungeon in Fez.

There in the Rif injustice was the daily bread. Everyone in the town knew what had happened, and everyone whispered. El Aroussi was a hero. The people were certain he would escape.

Time proved them right. Less than a year later the rumour was going around that he was in Tangier. Probably it did not reach the ears of Cheikh Abdeljbar. Perched above the town in his towers, he spoke only with men of importance, like himself.

The cheikh was ambitious. He hoped to marry his daughter Rahmana to the son of the Pacha of Slâ.

Included among his lands there was a castle on an estate in the Gharb, not far from Slâ, where he decided to take his family for a visit.

El Aroussi had indeed escaped from his confinement in Fez. He returned to his native town, where the people in the streets welcomed him, and commiserated with him for the unjust treatment he had received.

He listened impatiently, almost seeming not to hear them. He had grown bitter and silent. He was obliged to avenge himself against the cheikh. No other course of action was open to him. But the cheikh had gone to the Gharb.

As El Aroussi sat brooding one evening in his father's house, he came upon an idea as to how he might proceed. He knew it would be necessary for him to go and stay, perhaps for many months, in the vicinity of the castle near

Slâ, but having no access to money, he could see no way of keeping alive during the time of waiting. Now, however, he thought he had the solution.

The following morning he sought out his friends and put the question to them: would they be willing to go with him and live as bandits in the Forest of Mamora while they waited to carry out the attack upon Cheikh Abdeljbar?

In the end he recruited more than two dozen young men, all of them eager to help him clear his honour.

During the months while Cheikh Abdeljbar was making repeated visits to Slâ, as the arrangements for the forthcoming wedding slowly took form, El Aroussi and his friends lost no time in becoming the fiercest band of brigands in the region. The terror they caused throughout the Gharb was understandable, for they thought it safer to kill their victims before robbing them.

For generations the Forest of Mamora had been notorious as a robber-infested region. The outlaws raided the convoys of those unwise enough to pass within easy striking distance of the forest itself. If Cheikh Abdeljbar had spoken with the peasants working on his land, he might have been able to identify the new bandit chief from descriptions of his person in the gossip that was on everyone's lips. But the cheikh was far too busy in Slâ settling the bride-price with the pacha, and the details of the wedding-feast with his future son-in-law, Sidi Ali.

And Rahmana lay among the cushions swallowing pellets of almond paste with sesame and honey, while maidservants massaged her body with creams and oils.

Guests began to arrive at the castle several days before the wedding feast. On the final night the entire party, led by the bride and groom, set out on horseback in a torchlit procession for Slâ, where the festivities would be continued at the palace of the pacha when they arrived on the following day.

Their way led through a countryside of boulders and high cactus. The moon gave great clarity, and a cold sharp wind ran westward. There were songs, accompanied only by the hoofbeats of a hundred horses.

As they passed between the walls of a winding gorge, a great voice suddenly sounded from somewhere among the rocks nearby.

Ha huwa! El Aroussi!

There was a second's silence, and then the noise of thirty rifles firing into the procession from above.

In the stampede over the bodies of horses and men that followed, only the bridegroom was aware of the horseman who appeared from behind a boulder and rode straight at the bridal couple, at the last instant lifting Rahmana from her mount, and disappearing with her at a gallop into the night.

Cheikh Abdeljbar was unhurt. He and his son-in-law continued to Slâ and consulted with the pacha.

A few days later the Sultan sent soldiers to help the wronged father and husband. Cheikh Abdeljbar and Sidi Ali had taken a solemn oath to search for Rahmana until they found her.

On many occasions as they rode with the soldiers they had glimpses of the bandits just before they vanished into the depths of the forest. There were skirmishes in which both sides bore losses, but the leader was never seen among his henchmen.

It took more than a year for the soldiers to encircle the densest region of the forest. Those of El Aroussi's followers who were left had seen the danger in time and fled.

The weeks went by, while the Sultan's soldiers drew an always tightening ring around the part of the forest from which they were sure El Aroussi had not escaped.

It was Sidi Ali's dogs that finally led to his discovery. They found him in a cave by the edge of a stream, his body wasted with hunger, his face haggard and scarred.

They trussed him and took him to one of the tents at the campsite, where they dumped him onto the ground.

Then Sidi Ali squatted down, drew his dagger, and slowly amputated all ten of the captive's toes, tossing them one by one into El Aroussi's face.

When he had finished with this task, he withdrew to another tent to confer with Cheikh Abdeljbar on the form of death to provide for their prisoner the next morning.

They sat up half the night diverting themselves and each other with suggestions which grew increasingly more grotesque.

By the time the cheikh rose to retire to his own tent, he was in favour of cutting a horizontal line around El Aroussi's waist and then flaying him, pulling the skin upwards over his head and eventually twisting it around his neck to strangle him.

This did not seem sufficiently drastic to Sidi Ali, who thought it would be more fitting to cut off his ears and nose and force him to swallow them, then to slash open his stomach, pull them out and make him swallow them again, and so on, for as long as he remained alive.

The older man reflected for a moment. Then, wishing his son-in-law a pleasant night, he said that with Allah's consent they would continue their discussion in the morning.

The dialogue was never resumed. During the black hour before dawn, the cheikh awoke, frozen by the sound of a voice that cried: *Ha huwa!* El Aroussi!

The cheikh sprang up and rushed out. The prisoner's tent was empty. He ran to Sidi Ali's tent. The young man lay dead. A spear was buried in his eye.

61

As the cheikh stood staring down in disbelief, there was the sound of a horse's hoofbeats outside. They grew fainter and were gone. El Aroussi had mounted the cheikh's own steed and ridden off on it.

The next morning, after washing and burying Sidi Ali (for they could not carry his body as far as Slâ), Cheikh Abdeljbar and the soldiers set out once more in pursuit.

Before noon they met the horse walking slowly in their direction, its saddle and flanks smeared with blood. The cheikh dismounted and ran to get astride it, turning it and making it retrace its steps. The forest was dense and difficult to push through, but the animal seemed to know its way.

They came soon to a small clearing where a rude hut had been built. The door was open.

Cheikh Abdeljbar stood in the doorway, trying to see into the dark interior. El Aroussi lay supine on the floor. It was clear that he was dead.

Then the cheikh saw the girl crouching by the body, while she kissed the stumps of El Aroussi's toes, one by one. He called her name, already fearful that she would not respond.

She did not seem to hear her father's outcry. When he lifted her up to embrace her, she stared at him and drew away. The soldiers were obliged to bind her in order to get her out of the hut and onto the horse with her father.

Cheikh Abdeljbar took Rahmana back to the Castle of Mamora. He hoped that with the passage of time she would cease her constant calling out of El Aroussi's name.

One day when she was in the garden, she found a gate unlocked, and quickly stepped outside. What happened to her after that is a mystery, for she was not seen again. The people of the countryside claimed that she had returned to the forest in search of El Aroussi. They sang a song about her:

Days of less substance than the nights that slip
    between
And Rahmana wanders in the forest, and the branches
    catch her hair.

VIII

At night in the courtyards of the Rif, grandfathers fashion grenades. Each rock in the ravine shields a man. The Spaniard in the garrison starts from sleep, to find his throat already slashed.

At night the Légionnaires in the oasis, drunk with hot beer and self-pity, howl songs of praise for a distant homeland. The sand is cold under the branches of the tamarisks where the camels lie, shaded from the moonlight.

Ayayayay! Nothing good is going to come of this.
The Americans were here.
The people grew rich,
Most of all the women.
Even the hags tore off their veils
And filled their mouths with chewing-gum.
Men waited in vain for their wives.
Handsome faces and green eyes
Had spirited them away.
And the girls parted their hair
And wore French skirts.
They wanted to be with the Americans.
And you heard only *Hokay, hokay*.

The soldiers gave us cigarettes,
They gave us chocolates and dollars.
And even the oldest crones wore silk kerchiefs
When the Americans were here.
And *Hokay, hokay! Bye bye!*

They gave candy today and gum tomorrow.
The girls covered their faces
With powder made from chickpeas,
And they ate bonbons.

And even the hags sat drinking rum
With the Americans.
And you heard: *Hokay, hokay! Come on! Bye bye!*

Money for everybody.
It was the girls who brought it back.
They carried handbags.
They wanted to be with the Americans.
And all you could hear was *Hokay, hokay!*
Give me dollar. Come on! Bye bye!

At night the French police quietly block the entrances to the Mellah, claiming to fear friction between Moslems and Jews. And at night they quietly remove the protection, allowing the Moslems to enter the quarter and pillage it.

A certain night the air was heavy with jasmine, and the bodies of Frenchmen and their families were left lying along the roads, under the cypresses in the public gardens, among the smoking ruins of the little villas. While it was still dark, a breeze sprang up.

IX

When Spain ruled the Chemel, her officers liked to hunt for deer. The animals were few, and smaller than the ones they were used to hunting in Spain. Deer from the Pyrenees were sent repeatedly across the Mediterranean to Melilla, and turned loose in the mountains, where they flourished, and, mixing with the native herds, quickly produced a larger and stronger breed.

Under the Spanish the people of the Chemel could not own firearms. When the Spaniards went home and the Moroccans were left in charge, the law remained the same as before.

A time of trouble then began for people who lived in distant wooded areas. Reports of fatal accidents circulated through the countryside. In earlier days the stags had fled from the presence of men; now they often sought them out and attacked them, and the men had no means of defence.

Si Abdelaziz, a prosperous farmer of Tchar Serdioua, had four sons whose ages ranged from sixteen to twenty. They were still unmarried because in recent years he had been busy and had not taken the time to go out and find brides for them.

When he had a certain sum set by, he began to visit other villages in the region in order to pick out a girl for his eldest son.

Eventually, in a tchar some two hours' walk up the valley, he came to terms with the father of a girl. Si Abdelaziz was not able to see her himself, but he was assured by her family that she was in excellent health and in perfect condition for marriage.

After settling the details in the bride-price agreement, he paid the man and returned to Tchar Serdioua satisfied with the transaction.

To his first-born son Mohammed he said: You have a wife. The wedding feast will take place the seventh day after Mouloud.

From among the young men of the tchar the son chose his *wazzara*, who would paint the designs on his hands with henna, build the wall of canes and bushes in front of his father's house, and finally go to fetch the bride from her village.

The day before the wedding feast was to be celebrated, Mohammed and his *wazzara* still had not completed the wall. They worked from dawn to evening, and got it all finished save for one small section, which Mohammed said he would build himself after the others had gone to get the girl.

The procession set out up the valley a little after midnight, to the sound of rhaitas and drums. Si Abdelaziz, who accompanied it, said they would be back by daybreak.

There was a stream a short distance below the house, bordered on both sides by dense vegetation. Mohammed made several trips there, bringing back armfuls of green bushes to weave into the still unfinished wall. It was late by the time he had it all done. He ran down to the river once more to bathe and pray before lying down to await the arrival of the bridal party.

The women of the household were awakened by the

74

furious bellowing of a stag, a sound that everyone in the tchar had learned to dread. They called to Mohammed, but he did not answer. The men from a nearby farm had heard the animal's call, and they came running. As they approached Si Abdelaziz's house, the stag bellowed again.

First they saw Mohammed's white garments moving on the ground as the stag stamped on them and gored them with his antlers. Then they saw Mohammed lying on his side, with his intestines coiling out of him into the dirt. The stag bellowed once more, turned, and disappeared into the darkness. They carried the body up to the house and covered it.

It was growing light when the people of Tchar Serdioua first heard the sharp sounds of the wedding procession coming down the valley. A group of men ran up the road to meet it and give Si Abdelaziz the bad news. The procession arrived at the house in silence.

After Mohammed's burial the three younger sons conferred among themselves. They were of the opinion that the stag had come to kill Mohammed because it knew he was about to marry the girl. It followed that any man foolhardy enough to take her would very likely suffer the same fate.

Si Abdelaziz, having paid for the bride, had no intention of sending her home again. He called in the oldest of the three remaining sons and told him she was for him. The youth steadfastly refused to have her.

Si Abdelaziz tried the next son, and then the youngest, but neither would agree to accept her. The girl learned of this, and begged to be taken back to her village. In a fit of anger, the old man announced that he was marrying her himself.

The three youths refused to speak to their new mother-in-law. They were waiting for the stag. Each time their father went into the woods they listened for the killer's voice.

The stag never came. Si Abdelaziz died in bed a year later, and the girl was free to return as a widow to her own tchar.

X

The country of the Anjra is almost devoid of paved roads. It is a region of high jagged mountains and wooded valleys, and does not contain a town of any size. During the rainy season there are landslides. Then, until the government sends men to repair the damage, the roads cannot be used. All this is very much on the minds of the people who live in the Anjra, particularly when they are waiting for the highways to be rebuilt so that trucks can move again between the villages. Four or five soldiers had been sent several months earlier to repair the potholes along the road between Ksar es Seghir and Melloussa. Their tent was beside the road, near a curve in the river.

A peasant named Hattash, whose village lay a few miles up the valley, constantly passed by the place on his way to and from Ksar es Seghir. Hattash had no fixed work of any sort, but he kept very busy looking for a chance to pick up a little money one way or another in the market and the cafés. He was the kind of man who prided himself on his cleverness in swindling foreigners, by which he meant men from outside the Anjra. Since his friends shared his dislike of outsiders, they found his exploits amusing, although they were careful to have no dealings with him.

Over the months Hattash had become friendly with

the soldiers living in the tent, often stopping to smoke a pipe of kif with them, perhaps squatting down to play a few games of ronda. Thus when one day the soldiers decided to give a party, it was natural that they should mention it to Hattash, who knew everyone for miles around, and therefore might be able to help them. The soldiers came from the south, and their isolation there by the river kept them from meeting anyone who did not regularly pass their tent.

I can get you whatever you want, Hattash told them. The hens, the vegetables, oil, spices, salad, whatever.

Fine. And we want some girls or boys, they added.

Don't worry about that. You'll have plenty to choose from. What you don't want you can send back.

They discussed the cost of the party for an hour or so, after which the soldiers handed Hattash twenty-five thousand francs. He set off, ostensibly for the market.

Instead of going there, he went to the house of a nearby farmer and bought five of his best hens, with the understanding that if the person for whom he was buying them should not want them, he could return the hens and get his money back.

Soon Hattash was outside the soldiers' tent with the hens. How are they? he said. The men squeezed them and examined them, and pronounced them excellent. Good, said Hattash. I'll take them home now and cook them.

He went back to the farmer with the hens and told him that the buyer had refused them. The farmer shrugged and gave Hattash his money.

This seemed to be the moment to leave Ksar es Seghir, Hattash decided. He stopped at a café and invited everyone there to the soldiers' tent that evening, telling them there would be food, wine and girls. Then he bought bread, cheese and fruit, and began to walk along the trails that would lead him over the mountains to Khemiss dl

Anjra.

With the twenty-five thousand francs he was able to live for several weeks there in Khemiss dl Anjra. When he had come to the end of them, he began to think of leaving.

In the market one morning he met Hadj Abdallah, a rich farmer from Farsioua, which was a village only a few miles from his own. Hadj Abdallah, a burly, truculent man, always had eyed Hattash with distrust.

Ah, Hattash! What are you doing up here? It's a while since I've seen you.

And you? said Hattash.

Me? I'm on my way to Tetuan. I'm leaving my mule here and taking the bus.

That's where I'm going, said Hattash.

Well, see you in Tetuan, said Hadj Abdallah, and he turned, unhitched his mule, and rode off.

Khemiss dl Anjra is a very small town, so that it was not difficult for Hattash to follow along at some distance, and see the house where Hadj Abdallah tethered his mule and into which he then disappeared. He walked to the bus station and sat under a tree.

An hour or so later, when the bus was filling up with people, Hadj Abdallah arrived and bought his ticket. Hattash approached him.

Can you lend me a thousand francs? I haven't got enough to buy the ticket.

Hadj Abdallah looked at him. No, I can't, he said. Why don't you stay here? And he went and got into the bus.

Hattash, his eyes very narrow, sat down again under the tree. When the bus had left, and the cloud of smoke and dust had drifted off over the meadows, he walked back to the house where the Hadj had left his mule. She still stood there, so he quietly unhitched her, got astride her, and rode her in the direction of Mgas Tleta. He was still smarting under Hadj Abdallah's insult, and he vowed to give him as much trouble as he could.

Mgas Tleta was a small tchar. He took the mule to the fondaq and left it in charge of the guardian. Being ravenously hungry, he searched in his clothing for a coin or two to buy a piece of bread, and found nothing.

In the road outside the fondaq he caught sight of a peasant carrying a loaf in the hood of his djellaba. Unable to take his eyes from the bread, he walked towards the man and greeted him. Then he asked him if he had work, and was not surprised when the man answered no. He went on, still looking at the bread: If you want to earn a thousand francs, you can take my mule to Mdiq. My father's waiting for her and he'll pay you. Just ask for Si Mohammed Tsuli. Everybody in Mdiq knows him. He always has a lot of men working for him. He'll give you work there too if you want it.

The peasant's eyes lit up. He agreed immediately.

Hattash sighed. It's a long time since I've seen good country bread like that, he said, pointing at the loaf that emerged from the hood of the djellaba. The man took it out and handed it to him. Here. Take it.

In return Hattash presented him with the receipt for the mule. You'll have to pay a hundred francs to get her out of the fondaq, he told him. My father will give it back to you.

That's all right. The man was eager to start out for Mdiq.

Si Mohammed Tsuli. Don't forget.

No, no! Bslemah.

Hattash, well satisfied, watched the man ride off. Then he sat down on a rock and ate the whole loaf of bread. He had no intention of returning home to risk meeting the soldiers or Hadj Abdallah, so he decided to hide himself for a while in Tetuan, where he had friends.

When the peasant arrived at Mdiq the following day, he

found that no one could tell him where Si Mohammed Tsuli lived. He wandered back and forth through every street in the town, searching and inquiring. When evening came, he went to the gendarmerie and asked if he might leave the mule there. But they questioned him and accused him of having stolen the animal. His story was ridiculous, they said, and they locked him into a cell.

Not many days later Hadj Abdallah, having finished his business in Tetuan, went back to Khemiss dl Anjra to get his mule and ride her home. When he heard that she had disappeared directly after he had taken the bus, he remembered Hattash, and was certain that he was the culprit. The theft had to be reported in Tetuan, and much against his will he returned there.

Your mule is in Mdiq, the police told him.

Hadj Abdallah took another bus up to Mdiq.

Papers, said the gendarmes. Proof of ownership.

The Hadj had no documents of that sort. They told him to go to Tetuan and apply for the forms.

During the days while he waited for the papers to be drawn up, signed and stamped, Hadj Abdallah grew constantly angrier. He went twice a day to talk with the police. I know who took her! he would shout. I know the son of a whore.

If you ever catch sight of him, hold on to him, they told him. We'll take care of him.

Although Tetuan is a big place with many crowded quarters, the unlikely occurred. In a narrow passageway near the Souq el Fouqi late one evening Hadj Abdallah and Hattash came face to face.

The surprise was so great that Hattash remained frozen to the spot, merely staring into Hadj Abdallah's eyes. Then he heard a grunt of rage, and felt himself seized by the other man's strong arm.

Police! Police! roared Hadj Abdallah. Hattash squirmed,

but was unable to free himself.

One policeman arrived, and then another. Hadj Abdallah did not release his grip of Hattash for an instant while he delivered his denunciation. Then with an oath he struck his prisoner, knocking him flat on the sidewalk. Hattash lay there in the dark without moving.

Why did you do that? the policemen cried. Now you're the one who's going to be in trouble.

Hadj Abdallah was already frightened. I know. I ought not to have hit him.

It's very bad, said one policeman, bending over Hattash, who lay completely still. You see, there's blood coming out of his head.

A small crowd was collecting in the passageway.

There were only a few drops of blood, but the policeman had seen Hattash open one eye and had heard him whisper: Listen.

He bent over still farther, so that his ear was close to Hattash's lips.

He's got money, Hattash whispered.

The policeman rose and went over to Hadj Abdallah. We'll have to call an ambulance, he said, and you'll have to come to the police station. You had no right to hit him.

At that moment Hattash began to groan.

He's alive, at least! cried Hadj Abdallah. Hamdul'lah!

Then the policemen began to speak with him in low tones, advising him to settle the affair immediately by paying cash to the injured man.

Hadj Abdallah was willing. How much do you think? he whispered.

It's a bad cut he has on his head, the same policeman said, going back to Hattash. Come and look.

Hadj Abdallah remained where he was, and Hattash groaned as the man bent over him again. Then he murmured: Twenty thousand. Five for each of you.

When the policeman rejoined Hadj Abdallah, he told him the amount. You're lucky to be out of it.

Hadj Abdallah gave the money to the policeman, who took it over to Hattash and prodded him. Can you hear me? he shouted.

Ouakha, groaned Hattash.

Here. Take this. He held out the banknotes in such a way that Hadj Abdallah and the crowd watching could see them clearly. Hattash stretched up his hand and took them, slipping them into his pocket.

Hadj Abdallah glared at the crowd and pushed his way through, eager to get away from the spot.

After he had gone, Hattash slowly sat up and rubbed his head. The onlookers still stood there watching. This bothered the two policemen, who were intent on getting their share of the money. The recent disclosures of corruption, however, had made the public all too attentive at such moments. The crowd was waiting to see them speak to Hattash or, if he should move, follow him.

Hattash saw the situation and understood. He rose to his feet and quickly walked up the alley.

The policemen looked at each other, waited for a few seconds, and then began to saunter casually in the same direction. Once they were out of sight of the group of onlookers they hurried along, flashing their lights up each alley in their search. But Hattash knew the quarter as well as they, and got safely to the house of his friends.

He decided, however, that with the two policemen on the lookout for him Tetuan was no longer the right place for him, and that his own tchar in the Anjra would be preferable.

Once he was back there, he made discreet inquiries about the state of the road to Ksar es Seghir. The repairs were finished, his neighbours told him, and the soldiers had been sent to some other part of the country.

85

XI

The river runs fast at the mouth where the shore is made of the sky, and the wavelets curl inward fanwise from the sea. For the swimmer there is no warning posted against the sharks that enter and patrol the channel. Some time before sunset birds come to stalk or scurry along the sandbar, but before dark they are gone.

NOTES AND SOURCES

I

Topographical features mentioned by Hanno the Carthaginian are no longer in existence. The Atlantic coastline of Morocco has greatly altered in the past twenty-four centuries.

II

A *fondouq* (p. 18) is a caravanserai where travellers may find accommodation for themselves and stabling for their horses, donkeys or mules.

Mention of a King Mohammed VIII in the early sixteenth century may cause surprise to those who remember that King Mohammed V died in 1961. Altogether thirteen monarchs bore the name before the establishment of the present dynasty in 1649, at which point the enumeration was begun afresh.

Passio gloriosi martyris beati fratris Andreae de Spoleto, ordinis minorum regularis observantiae p. catholico fidei veritate passi in Affrica civitate Fez, Anno 1532, Tolosoae (in verse).

(Translation into Spanish published at Medina del Campo in 1543, entitled *Tesauro de virtudes copilado por un religioso portuguez, Sigue el Martyro de Fr. Andres de Espoleto en Fez.*)

IV

The incident is mentioned in *The Empire of Morocco* by James Grey Jackson (William Bulmer & Co., London, 1809).

V

Djenoun (singular *djinn*; p. 46) are fearsome spirits capable of assuming human or animal form.

91

VI

The *ulema* (p. 53) constitute a council of men versed theoretically and practically in the laws of Islam, holding government appointments in a Moslem state.

Mokhaznia (p. 53) are military guards.

El Martirio de la joven Hachuel, la Heroina Hebrea by Eugenio Maria Romero (Gibraltar, 1837).

Reference is made to the occurrence in the *Times of Morocco*, 25 September, 1888. Also in *Archives Israélites*, Vol. XLI, Nos. 22-24, 1880.

A play based on the case, by Antonio Calle, was published in Seville in 1852.

VII

The tale appears in *Morocco* by Edmondo de Amicis (Henry T. Coates & Co., Philadelphia, 1897).

VIII

A literal translation of the lyrics of a popular song in Moghrebi Arabic of the 1950s.

IX

Spanish rule in Morocco terminated with Independence, in 1956. The difficulties recounted took place during the 'sixties and 'seventies.

X

A *fondaq* (p. 82) is a hotel. During the French occupation, *fondouq* and *fondaq* were used interchangeably to mean 'hostelry'; present-day usage distinguishes between a *fondouq* - a caravanserai where animals are accommodated - and a *fondaq*, a hotel.

This episode occurred in 1980.